This book
belongs to

- - - - - - - - - - - - - - - - - -

- - - - - - - - - - - - - - - - - -

Little Grey Rabbit's

YEAR OF STORIES

Little Grey Rabbit's

YEAR OF STORIES

By Alison Uttley
Illustrated by Margaret Tempest

templar publishing

Contents

Little Grey Rabbit and Alison Uttley 8

Spring

Hare and the Easter Eggs 15
Little Grey Rabbit's May Day 41

Summer

Little Grey Rabbit Goes to the Sea 69
Water Rat's Picnic 95

Autumn

Fuzzypeg Goes to School............................123

Winter

Little Grey Rabbit's Christmas 151

Little Grey Rabbit and Alison Uttley

Alison Uttley published her first Little Grey Rabbit book in 1929. Based on a brilliantly imagined community of animals with homely, sensible Little Grey Rabbit, vain and selfish Squirrel and the boastful and adventurous Hare at their centre, these little books, beautifully and sensitively illustrated by Margaret Tempest, were soon selling in their hundreds of thousands, making their author, Alison Uttley, a household name.

With a varied and supporting cast of characters, including Moldy Warp the mole, Fuzzypeg the little hedgehog, Wise Owl, Water Rat, the Speckledy Hen and many more, the thirty or so tales describe the everyday life and the adventures, trials and dilemmas of their woodland characters, upon whom the occasional swooping danger descends and is contained by a mixture of good sense, togetherness and courage.

Alison Uttley was convinced that children loved the Little Grey Rabbit characters 'because I believe in them. Mine aren't made up, they're real…I was born in a place of beauty…I talked to all the animals'. Brought up as the unusually gifted daughter of a tenant farmer and his wife in the hilly Derbyshire countryside, Alison was indeed surrounded by animals on her beloved and remote Castle Top Farm and those in the surrounding woods and fields. She felt that animals 'have such a raw deal, and I think they are very faithful and very, very patient.'

She wrote: 'In these little books I always try to give some specially English touch of country life, which might [otherwise] be forgotten.' More than this, Alison was a passionate observer of the changing seasons and of the swirling constellations in the night skies. She made a point of bowing to the new moon to bring her luck. She greeted the month of her birth, December, 'the new month, the month I love, with a kiss.' She thought of herself as 'a snow-baby, a lucky baby, they said, born just before Christmas, in the great storm.' We learn from her diaries that the month of April was also a favourite to be welcomed like a lost child or lover: 'Lovely darling April has come. I ran down to open the door to let her in yesterday.'

It is small wonder, then, that in the Little Grey Rabbit books the seasons, the stars, the moon and the sun, the contours and the flora and fauna of the traditional English countryside are celebrated with such tenderness and with so keen an eye.

Denis Judd
London
2015

The latest edition of Professor Denis Judd's authorised biography, Alison Uttley: Spinner of Tales *was published in 2010; he is also editor of her diaries,* The Private Diaries of Alison Uttley, 1932–1971, *paperback 2011.*

Spring

In Spring, Little Grey Rabbit sees daffodils
and bluebells come out of the earth and
celebrates Easter with chocolate eggs.

Summer

On hot summer days, Little Grey Rabbit
and her friends love riverside picnics and sand
and shells at the seaside.

Autumn

In Autumn, the leaves are changing colour
and it's time for little animals like Fuzzypeg
the Hedgehog to go to school.

Winter

Winter brings snow and sleigh rides and cosy nights
by the fire. On Christmas Eve, Little Grey Rabbit
hangs up her Christmas stocking.

Spring

Hare and the
Easter Eggs

ONE EVENING IN SPRING, Hare was dancing along the fields, skipping and tripping and bowing to the rabbits. It was the month of March and he was feeling excited and wild, for all hares are mad in March.

"I'll go to the village," said he. "I'll go and see what there is to be seen and tell them at home all about it. I feel very brave tonight."

He stuck a primrose in his coat for luck and a cowslip in his collar for bravery, and he cut a hazel switch with catkins dangling from it, just in case.

"I'll look at the village shop and see if Mrs Bunting and the shop-bell are still there."

It was dusk when he reached the village and the children were indoors having tea. Not even a dog or cat was to be seen. Hare leapt softly and swiftly down the cobbled street.

He gave a chirrup of joy when he saw that the shop was still open. Jars of sweets in the window shone with many colours in the light of the lamp.

Hare crept close. It was a lovely sight! Whips and tops, dolls and toy horses, cakes and buns were there.

Then he opened his eyes very wide, for he saw something strange. On a dish lay a pile of chocolate eggs with sugary flowers and 'Happy Easter' written on them. Ribbons were tied round them in blue, pink and yellow bows.

"Eggs! 'Normous eggs!" whispered Hare.

He stared and licked his lips. "What kind of hen lays these pretty eggs? I should like to take Grey Rabbit one, and Squirrel one and me one."

He pressed closer to the glass and his long ears flapped against the pane. Just then footsteps came down the street, and he slipped into the shadows and crouched there dark as night. His fur quivered, and his heart thumped.

A woman stopped at the shop window, so close to Hare that her skirt brushed his ears. She lifted the door latch and pushed open the door. A loud tinkle-tinkle came from the bell hanging above it.

"The bell's telling who comes into the shop," thought Hare.

"Good evening, Mrs Bunting," called the woman. "Those are nice Easter eggs. How much are they?"

"A shilling each, Mrs Snowball," replied Mrs Bunting, and she set the dish on the counter.

Hare crept into the shop and stood by Mrs Snowball's skirts with his nose raised, sniffing the sweet smells of chocolate and new bread.

Mrs Snowball chose her egg and, as the two women chatted, Hare stretched out a furry paw, took a leap, and snatched a chocolate egg. In a moment he was gone, out into the dusk.

"Oh! Oh!" cried Mrs Bunting. "What was that? Something took an egg!"

"I didn't see anything," said Mrs Snowball.

They both ran to the shop door, but Hare was already far away, running like the wind.

"You can't catch me," he laughed. He stopped to look at the egg. His warm fur had softened the chocolate and his fist went through. He brought out a little fluffy chicken made of silk and wool.

Hare licked his paws and then licked the egg.

"Oh! De-larcious!" he cried, and soon the egg disappeared.

"That's the best egg I've ever tasted," said he, and he galloped across the common and dashed into the little house where Grey Rabbit was cooking the supper.

"Here you come at last, Hare," cried Squirrel. "What have you been eating? You are brown and dirty."

"Not dirt, Squirrel, it's chocolate," panted Hare. "You'll never guess! I've eaten an egg laid by an Easter hen and it was made of chocolate," he said proudly.

"Nonsense," snapped Squirrel.

"Chocolate egg?" cried Grey Rabbit. "Where was it?"

"In the village shop," said Hare. "I took it right under the nose of Mrs Bunting. I shall go and pay for it," explained Hare. "It was a shilling."

"You took an egg and you ate it all yourself," said Squirrel. "Greedy Hare!"

"I brought you the ribbon, Squirrel, and the little fluffy chicken inside the egg is for Grey Rabbit," said Hare.

All evening they talked of Easter eggs.

The next morning, after breakfast, the three set off for Wise Owl's house. They couldn't wait till night, so they had to wake the Owl from his sleep. They rang the little silver bell and they stood in a row under the tree waiting for him.

"Who's there?" hooted Wise Owl very crossly. "Go away or I'll eat you."

"Please, Wise Owl…" began Grey Rabbit, waving her handkerchief for a truce.

"We want to know…" added Squirrel, stammering with fright.

"About Easter eggs," shouted Hare in a loud voice. "Chocolate ones."

"And who lays them," whispered Grey Rabbit.

"I've got a good mind to tell you nothing," said Wise Owl, frowning at the noisy Hare. "But remembering the primrose wine, and thinking of eggs you will bring me, I'll speak."

"Yes, Wise Owl," said Grey Rabbit meekly.
"Hoots and toots," snorted Hare.

"Easter eggs come at Easter, for children and good Rabbits but not for Hares," said Wise Owl.

"The church bells ring, and the little birds sing, and the sun dances on Easter morning."

He blinked and yawned and went to bed, banging his door so that the bough shook.

Grey Rabbit and Squirrel went home, but Hare leapt aside and ran across the fields. He tapped on Mole's door.

"Moldy Warp? Quick! Are you at home?" he called.

"What's the hurry, Hare?" asked the Mole.

"Can you lend me a silver penny, or a gold penny or anything?" Hare asked.

"What's it for, Hare?"

"For a secret, a fine secret. I owe a silver penny and if you could give me an extra one…" said Hare.

Moldy Warp went into his underground house and brought up a fistful of gold coins.

"You can have these if you'll do something for me," said he.

"Oh, thank you, Moldy Warp. You are a real friend," cried Hare stuffing the coins in his pocket.

"I have a fancy for some eggs," said Moldy Warp.

"I'll bring you some at once," said Hare, gladly. "I'll go to old Speckledy Hen."

Speckledy Hen was in the meadow, scratching among the daisies when Hare came up.

"Please, Speckledy Hen, can I have some eggs for Moldy Warp?" asked Hare.

"I wanted to give Grey Rabbit my eggs," said the Hen. "Why should I send them to the Mole?"

"He wants them very special," said Hare. "Do please let me have them, Speckledy Hen."

"Very well. As it's nearly Easter, I will," said the Hen. She filled a basket from the store of eggs in the barn.

"These have been laid by my friends, but my own egg is for Grey Rabbit."

Hare carried the eggs to Mole.

"I'm going to be very busy," said Moldy Warp. "I'm getting ready for Easter."

He carried the eggs indoors and shut the door.

"I've got a secret, a secret, a secret," sang Hare, leaping towards home.

When he got to the little house he kept jingling the coins in his pocket.

"What makes that jingle-jangle in your pocket, Hare?" asked Squirrel.

"It's a secret," said Hare. He took out his watch and shook it and altered the fingers to make the time pass more quickly.

"I'm going out again tonight," he announced.

"You'll take care, won't you?" asked Grey Rabbit.

As soon as tea was over he went to the village, for he wanted another look at the Easter eggs.

Hare had some difficulty in getting to the shop, for children were looking in at the window. He had to wait until they went away, and when all was safe he darted across the road.

"I'll wait till somebody comes along and Mrs Bunting opens the door."

Hare leaned against the door, but it was not fastened, and his fat little body fell inside the shop.

"Tinkle! Tinkle! Tinkle!" rang the little bell.

"Oh dear!" cried Hare.

Mrs Bunting heard the jingling bell, but she stopped to take the kettle off the fire in the back room. That gave Hare his chance. He dived into a brown jug which stood near.

"Drat those children! They're after my Easter eggs," said Mrs Bunting. "Well, it's time to shut up shop."

She locked and bolted the door. She took the money from the till and turned down the lamp. Then she went to the back room and shut the door.

Hare stood on his head in the jug. He heard the sounds of door and shutters, but he was too busy trying not to sneeze to bother about them.

Slowly he pushed up his long ears, his round head and his astonished eyes. There, watching him, sat a fine tabby cat. The two stared hard at each other.

"Good evening," said Hare, and he scrambled out and made a deep bow.

"Gracious me!" exclaimed the Tabby. "Pleased to meet you, Mister Hare."

"At your service, ma'am," said Hare politely.

"What are you doing here? It isn't safe," said the Cat.

"I'm here to pay a debt," said Hare.

"Hist!" cried the Cat, and Hare leapt back in the jug as the door opened and Mrs Bunting appeared.

"Come along Puss," she said.

"Miaow! Miaow!" cried the Cat, retreating to a corner.

"Oh, very well! Perhaps there's a mouse," said Mrs Bunting. She fetched a saucerful of milk and shut the door.

"You can come out now," whispered the Cat. "She'll go to bed soon."

Hare climbed out clutching the gold coins.

"I've come to buy some Easter eggs," said he. "Here's the money."

"This will buy up the shop," said the Cat. "We never see any gold, only shillings and pennies."

Mrs Bunting's footsteps thudded up the stairs into the bedroom over the shop.

"Now we can talk," said the Cat with relief. "I want to hear about you and Squirrel and Grey Rabbit. I'll get you a bite to eat first."

She fetched some sausages and ham from the counter and sugary buns from the window.

"Eat these, Hare," said she, and Hare gobbled them up.

He told all his adventures and many more, and the Cat thought he was the bravest, boldest animal she had ever met.

The evening wore on, the moon peered through a chink in the shutters and smiled at the sight of these two together.

Wise Owl came hooting over the roof, and Hare told about him. The Fox came snuffling outside and Hare told about him too. The Weasels squeaked as they ran down the street and Hare told of them and their tricks.

Then his head nodded, and he slept.

Dawn came with the crowing of cocks and Hare opened his eyes.

"It's time you were off, Hare," said the Cat. "I'll open the door for you."

Hare packed the Easter eggs in a basket while the Cat unlocked the door. She wrapped a duster round the chattering tongue of the little bell and opened the door.

Hare poured his gold coins on the dish, and seized the basket of eggs.

"Goodbye, Mistress Tabby," said he. "Thank you very much for your kindness."

"Miaow! Miaow!" answered the Cat.

Hare didn't wait any longer.

Hare hid the chocolate eggs in the empty beehive, and then he crept into bed.

"Would you like an Easter egg party?" asked Grey Rabbit after breakfast the next morning. "We will invite our dear friends to see the sun dance on Easter morning."

"Oh yes," cried Squirrel.

So Grey Rabbit made a heap of tiny cakes, each in the shape of a moon. Squirrel and Hare scribbled the invitations on primrose petals. Squirrel was a poor writer and Hare couldn't spell, so they put the letter E and nothing else.

Squirrel had knitted an egg for Grey Rabbit. She made it of blue wool and she stuffed it with nuts.

On Easter morning Grey Rabbit, Squirrel and Hare went to the garden in the early light. Hare was very excited about something. Grey Rabbit wondered why he kept looking at the beehive.

"We haven't any bees, Hare," she reminded him.

Footsteps came pattering down the lane and little voices could be heard singing songs.

"We didn't invite all these," whispered Squirrel.

"Please, Grey Rabbit, we've come to wish you a Happy Easter," said the small creatures of the woodland in shrill chorus. "A Happy Easter."

"A Happy Easter," replied Grey Rabbit.

Away in the east the sky was bathed in golden light, and rosy clouds floated above the rising sun.

All the animals gazed into the sky, and they saw the great ball of the sun come up from behind the hills, and dance that Easter morning.

Then Moldy Warp brought his basket of coloured eggs.

"These are magical eggs," said Grey Rabbit. "How ever did you make them, Moldy Warp?"

Rat came forward with a little bone egg which opened. Grey Rabbit opened it and found a wooden thimble and a few thorn pins.

"How clever of you to carve this little Easter egg!" said Grey Rabbit.

Squirrel offered her queer knitted egg, crooked and fat, and Grey Rabbit hugged her friend.

Next, old Hedgehog and Fuzzypeg came with duck eggs, and the Speckledy Hen brought her own new-laid egg.

All this time Hare had been dodging backwards and forwards, glancing at the beehive, and then going away. At last he lifted the straw skep and brought out the chocolate eggs.

"Grey Rabbit, Squirrel, Hedgehog family, Speckledy Hen, Moldy Warp, and all, I wish you a Happy Easter," said he.

On the grass he spread the chocolate eggs with their bright ribbons and curly lettering, and everybody cried out in surprise and pleasure.

Wise Owl, flying over, dived down and seized an egg. He pierced it with his beak and brought out the fluffy toy chick.

"Bah! A trick!" he snorted, and away he flew.

Hare mopped his forehead.

"Where did these come from?" Grey Rabbit asked.

"I bought them," said Hare. "Moldy Warp gave me the money. They are from Moldy Warp and me."

Moldy Warp looked surprised, and he stroked one of the eggs.

"Soft as velvet, sweet as honey," said he. "Bought with Roman gold, these eggs."

They sat on the ground in a circle and drank tiny glasses of primrose wine and ate bits of the Easter eggs.

"A Happy Easter," they said to one another, holding high their glasses.

Hare told his adventure, and they all thought he was a very clever Hare.

"Of course I am," said Hare. "I've been telling you for years, but you wouldn't believe me."

Little Grey Rabbit's May Day

"IT'S MAY DAY TOMORROW," announced Hare at breakfast time one morning. "There's going to be dancing round the Maypole in the village. The Maypole is set up with fine ribbons hanging down. I danced round last night when the children had gone to bed!"

"Hare! Did you? In the moonlight?" cried Grey Rabbit, astonished.

"Yes, all alone by the light of the moon," laughed Hare.

"I tried to bring you a ribbon but they were fastened out of my reach."

"Could we have a Maypole, Grey Rabbit?' asked Squirrel.

"We'll dance round the May tree, and that's better than a Maypole," said Grey Rabbit. "There's a lovely May tree in the field with blossom coming out already."

"Let's have a procession like the children in the village,' said Hare, leaping up with excitement. "They carry crowns and sceptres."

"Let me think," said Grey Rabbit. And she put her paw to her head and stood very still.

"We must gather lots of flowers early on May morning," she said, "with May dew on their petals. I'll take a jug to catch some May dew, for it's magical."

"Who is May?" asked Squirrel.

"May is the spirit of Spring," said Grey Rabbit. "I think I must ask Wise Owl about all this."

So away they went after the breakfast things were washed to find Wise Owl.

On the way, Hedgehog and Moldy Warp joined them.

"May Day?" asked Wise Owl, sleepily, looking down at them. "How to keep May Day? You ought to know. May is the Queen of the flowers. She's invisible, but you hang crowns and sceptres on a May tree and she will find them – a crown of flowers and a sceptre and cowslip balls."

"What kind of flowers, Wise Owl?" called Hare.

"Spring flowers, but at the top of the crown there must be a Crown Imperial," Owl answered.

"Does it grow in the woods?" "Is it wild or tame?" They all talked at once.

Wise Owl shook his head, but Moldy Warp spoke up. "I once saw the Crown Imperial. It had golden bells with a green topknot of leaves."

"Then I've seen it in the village,' said Old Hedgehog slowly. "In Miss Susan's garden."

Hare leapt up. "I've seen it too," he shouted. "When Miss Susan taught me to make lace. I was looking out of the corner of my eye and I saw a tall yellow lily."

"You'd better get one from the old Lady", said Hedgehog.

"Yes I will," said Hare.

"What can I do?" asked Fuzzypeg, who joined his father on the way home.

"You can make cowslip balls, Fuzzypeg. You know where cowslips grow," said Grey Rabbit.

"All of you can make sceptres on May morning," she said to the others as they hurried back home.

On May morning, as soon as the bright sun peeped from the horizon, the small animals came from their cottages and ran to the fields and hedgebanks to gather their fresh petals.

Grey Rabbit carried a tiny jug for May dew and Squirrel had a basket for flowers, but Hare was impatient to discover the Crown Imperials in the village street.

Moldy Warp shut his door and stepped across the dewy field. The wind was playing in the trees, and the beech leaves waved up and down.

He went to a willow by the stream and began to cut young branches with his little axe.

Then Grey Rabbit, Squirrel and Hare came up.

"A happy May Day," they called. "Why are you getting withies?" they asked.

"Why? Because you must have a foundation for the crowns and garlands you are going to make," said he. He stripped off the tender leaves and twined the slender branches to make hoops.

"You fasten the flowers to these," he explained.

"I'm going to the village to get the Crown Imperials," said Hare.

"You can't just go and take Miss Susan's precious flowers without asking," objected Grey Rabbit.

"Give her a cowslip ball,' suggested Squirrel.

Little Fuzzypeg was sitting near them with a basket of cowslips. By his side lay two beautiful cowslip balls, even and round.

"Can I have one for Miss Susan?" asked Grey Rabbit, stooping to admire his work. She picked up a ball and smelled its honey scent and tossed it and caught it.

"Yes," said the little Hedgehog. "I like her. She is very kind to little animals."

"I've got a hanky made of cobweb," said Grey Rabbit.
"I've got a walnut shell with nothing in it," said Squirrel, and she held out an empty shell.

"Fill it with new-mown hay," said Grey Rabbit.

So Squirrel picked some white starry flowers, and filled the little box. She tied the walnut's lid with green grasses, and it made a scent box for Miss Susan.

"I've got something at home for the old Lady," said Moldy Warp. "I'll go back to my cupboard where I keep my bits and bobs."

Hare scampered by the side of the slow-plodding Mole.

"Not much time to waste," said he as he leapt round his friend. "I must get those Crown Imperials before the village wakes up."

"Go and pick flowers for the garlands. I can't hurry any faster. I won't be long," said Mole.

Moldy Warp unlocked his door and disappeared in his dark house. He went to the cupboard in the earthy wall.

"I could give her an arrowhead,' he pondered, stroking a grey stone, "or a Roman penny."

He turned over coins, arrowheads and little stone lamps.

Then he pounced on something and took it to the light. It was a tiny bottle, green as grass, square and squat.

"This'll do. I'll fill it with dew from Grey Rabbit's jug, and it will make Miss Susan young again."

Moldy Warp took a carved bone pin with a hare on top, and put it with the bottle.

He tossed the rest of the things back in the cupboard, and went out to the impatient Hare.

"Hullo, Moldy Warp. I thought you were going to stay all day," said Hare. "What have you got?"

"Never you mind," said Moldy Warp, and he trotted back twice as fast, eager to show his finds to everyone.

He looked important as he drew his treasures out of his velvet pocket, and the animals left their crowns to look.

"Here's a Roman bottle they kept their tears in," said he. "We'll put some of Grey Rabbit's May dew into it."

"Yes, I gathered it from the May-blossom as soon as the sun's rays shone on it. It's magical," said Grey Rabbit.

"If Miss Susan puts a drop of it on her eyes she will see more clearly and need no spectacles," said Moldy Warp.

"A drop on her cheeks will make the wrinkles vanish, and give her new strength."

So very carefully Moldy Warp filled the tiny green bottle from Grey Rabbit's jug of May dew and Hare stuffed hawthorn in the top for a cork.

Moldy Warp held up the bone pin. "It's a Roman pin to fasten up her dress," said he.

"Now go off, Hare, and take all these presents and the cowslip ball. Miss Susan will gladly give you a Crown Imperial," they told him, and away he galloped.

In his big pockets he carried the Roman bottle, the walnut shell filled with new-mown hay and the cobweb handkerchief. On his arm dangled the cowslip ball, sweet as honey.

But Hare was late. The children, too, had been up at dawn, putting the finishing touches on their crowns and sceptres, and at the top of each crown was a fine Crown Imperial. Hare glanced at them uneasily.

"I hope they've left me one or two," he muttered as he dashed down the road to Miss Susan's cottage.

Yes, there under the wall of the cottage was a row of fine golden flowers, each with five bells and a green topknot.

"Please, Miss Susan!" cried Hare, as he banged on the door with his furry fists. Nobody answered. Miss Susan was not well, her eyes were tired, her worn hands were weary.

"Miss Susan," called Hare urgently.

But Miss Susan lay in her bed, half-dreaming.

"A happy May Day," squeaked Hare through the key-hole.

"Same to you," murmured Miss Susan. Then she started. "Who can it be? A mouse?" she asked herself. "One of the children? Do they want some Crown Imperials for their May Day?"

She listened, but there was no patter of feet, only a rustle as Hare slipped among the tall lilies.

"Who's there?" she called.

"It's only Hare," squeaked Hare, but she could not hear his high voice.

Hare cut two lilies, panting as he bit through the thick stalks, looking around nervously as footsteps came near.

"He went in here!" said a boy's voice.

Hare hurriedly dropped his presents where the Crown Imperials had grown – the tiny Roman tear bottle filled with the dew of May, the Roman pin with a hare on top, the walnut shell stuffed with new-mown hay, the little lace handkerchief – but the cowslip ball he hung on the door knob.

Then, clutching the golden flowers, he leapt down the steps and away.

"Catch him! A hare's been taking Miss Susan's lilies," the children cried as they tore after him. But nobody can catch a hare at full gallop, and Hare got safely away.

Later, Miss Susan dressed slowly and looked out at the children as they passed her door with their crowns and garlands.

"Miss Susan, Miss Susan," they called. "There was a hare in your garden this morning, early. He took your Crown Imperials."

"Whatever did he want with my flowers?" wavered Miss Susan sadly, as she saw her broken lily stems.

"I wish my flowers had gone to make a crown," she said, and she turned away.

Then she stopped, for she saw the cowslip ball hanging on the door knob.

Then something among the lily leaves caught her eye. She picked up the walnut and inside were the flowers of new-mown hay. She found the handkerchief of cobweb and the bone-carved pin with the hare on the top. She stooped down and picked up the little green bottle of ancient glass, with its stopper of hawthorn.

She sniffed at it and poured a drop on her hands, and rubbed a little on her aching head and eyes. Her headache vanished, and she could see the feathers of the birds, the petals of the flowers. Her eyes sparkled, her face was fresh and young again.

"Where did these things come from? Not from the children. This hanky is a fairy thing."

Then Miss Susan remembered the children said a hare had been in the garden. A hare!

"Once I taught a hare to make lace. Yes, that's it. On May Day anything might happen."

Away in the pasture another little procession was forming. Grey Rabbit fastened the Crown Imperial to the top of the lovely crown, made of cowslips, bluebells and forget-me-nots.

"There was a doll in the crown I saw," said Hare. They looked at one another.

"I haven't a doll," said Grey Rabbit. "Nor me. Nor me," said Squirrel and Fuzzypeg.

"I can make a doll for you," said Rat. He picked up a bit of oak and shaped it with his teeth so that there appeared a pretty little figure.

"How clever you are, Rat," said Grey Rabbit.

On its head she put a crown of May-blossom, and in its hand a bluebell wand. So the flowery doll sat in the middle of the crown, under the great Crown Imperial.

Grey Rabbit and Squirrel slung the crown on a hazel stick and carried it between them. Hare walked in front with a tall Crown Imperial sceptre. Fuzzypeg followed after with two cowslip balls. Then came Mr Hedgehog and Mrs Hedgehog with a smaller crown of May-blossom.

Moldy Warp followed with a sceptre of crab-apple blossom, and the little hedgehogs, Bill and Tim, walked with a garland of May and bluebells.

As they went their winding way to the old hawthorn, the animals sang their own May song:

May, May, we sing to the May
To sun and moon and Milky Way,
To field and wood and growing hay.
Grey Rabbit and Hare, Squirrel and all,
Fuzzypeg with his cowslip ball,
We carry the crown for beautiful May,
May Day. The First of May.

They hung the crowns and sceptres on the May tree, and then they danced around. The May tree rustled her branches and sent waves of perfume up into the blue sky, while all the birds came flying to the tree to join in the song of welcome.

At night, when everybody was fast asleep, Wise Owl flew over the May tree. It shone like silver, and in its branches hung the crown of flowers.

"Too whit. Too whoo, Happy May to you," called Wise Owl.

A silvery answer seemed to come from the tree.

"May Day, May Day," sang the tree, and Wise Owl shivered with delight.

Summer

Little Grey Rabbit Goes to the Sea

Squirrel had a cold, Hare had a cough and Grey Rabbit had the sneezes. It was all because Hare lost the key of the house one rainy night.

Grey Rabbit went to visit Mrs Hedgehog and Squirrel was left at home with Hare to take care of the house

"Let's go out too, Squirrel," pleaded Hare. "There are moonshadows and mushrooms and moldy warps all over the place. We shall get back home before Grey Rabbit."

"Lock the door and take the key," said Squirrel, and they ran away together, skipping under the cloudy sky, dancing in the fairy circles.

But the rain came down and Squirrel's tail was soon soaked, and Hare's fur was bedraggled. They were both wet and shivering. When they got home Grey Rabbit was waiting on the doorstep.

"A-tishoo!" said she.

"A-tishoo!" replied Hare and Squirrel.

"I think I've got a cold," said Grey Rabbit.

"I've got a cold too," said Squirrel. "A-tishoo!"

"I've got two colds," boasted Hare. "A-tishoo! A-tishoo!"

"Where's the key?" asked Grey Rabbit.

Hare felt in his pockets, he picked up the doormat, but there was nothing. They all hunted in the pouring rain, until at last Grey Rabbit found the little key by the garden gate.

How wet they were! Next morning they all had sore throats and bad colds.

"My missus will come over and look after you," said Milkman Hedgehog when Grey Rabbit sneezed on the doorstep.

So they all stayed in bed and Mrs Hedgehog came to nurse them.

They drank coltsfoot tea and sucked butterscotch. Little Fuzzypeg came with a bucket of soup. Mole sent a bunch of fragrant wild thyme. Water Rat brought a pot of lily-bud jam, and Speckledy Hen sent three eggs.

"What they want is a change of air," muttered poor Mrs Hedgehog as she trotted about.

Moldy Warp agreed with her.

"Come and stay underground with me," he invited them. "Nice dark damp house."

"Your house is too stuffy," said Hare, rudely.
"Dear Moldy Warp," said Grey Rabbit. "Your house is very nice, but we are used to sunshine."

"Change of air," advised Water Rat. "Come and live on the river and swim every day with me."

"Oh no," shivered Squirrel. "Too wet."

Wise Owl flew over one night and heard the sneezes. "What's all this atishooing?" he asked. "Squirrel, Hare and Grey Rabbit all got colds? They ought to have a day at the sea."

Nobody answered, but the little animals were listening.

"Too-whit! Too-whee! The beautiful sea," hooted Wise Owl, and he flew away.

"What is the sea?" asked Hare the next day. Squirrel and Grey Rabbit were not sure, but Fuzzypeg knew, for he went to school.

"It's water. Lots of water," said he. "The sea is salt."

"I don't like water," grumbled Hare. "Or salt."

Grey Rabbit put on her cloak that evening and went to ask Wise Owl about colds and sneezes.

"A day at the sea," advised Wise Owl.

"Where is the sea?" asked Grey Rabbit, but Wise Owl flew into his bedroom chuckling and hooting:

> *You'll get rid of your sneezes*
> *When you feel the sea breezes.*
> *Too-whit! Too-whee!*
> *The beautiful sea.*

"Silly Old Owl," exclaimed Squirrel, sneezing again.

Moldy Warp was more helpful when Grey Rabbit asked his advice.

"There's a blue caravan on the common," said he.
"It belongs to a brown horse, called Duke and a gipsy man.
Duke will take you to the sea."

"But-but who will drive?" asked Hare.

"Can't you drive a horse, Hare?" asked Mole. "Just hold the reins and sing out 'Gee-up, Duke'."

So Hare ran to all his special friends to invite them to go to the sea in a caraven.

Mr and Mrs Hedgehog accepted at once, and Fuzzypeg clapped his paws. Water Rat said he would be delighted, and even the Mole and the Speckledy Hen decided to go.

Everybody got ready. Squirrel made a little tent and Grey Rabbit packed a hamper of food. Hare fetched a spade and bucket. Moldy Warp put a golden guinea in his pocket.

The next morning, as soon as the sun rose, the three little animals set off. "A-tishoo. A-tishoo. A-tishoo!" they sneezed, as they ran over the fields to the common.

The Hedgehog family waited by the caravan, with Water Rat and the Speckledy Hen and Moldy Warp.

The old horse showed them the key and they unlocked the door of the caravan. Then with Hare and Moldy Warp and Squirrel on the front seat, and the rest of the animals inside, they started.

"Gee-up!" cried Hare, shaking the reins.

Inside the caravan Grey Rabbit, with the Hedgehog family, Water Rat and Speckledy Hen, explored. They jumped on the bed, and looked in the mirror. Grey Rabbit made a cup of tea and they ate a few crumbs of biscuit.

The caravan went through villages, past farms and cottages, down leafy lanes, in the quiet dawn. The horse chose the byways where they met nobody except a few wandering animals.

After a time everyone fell asleep, rocked by the motion of the swinging caravan. The old horse jogged along peacefully, for he knew every step of the way. He came at last to a lane which led to the grassy top of the cliffs, and at the end of this green path he stopped.

"Here we are," he neighed.

Hare tumbled off his seat down to the grass, and with him fell Squirrel and Mole, who were wrapped in the rug.

"The sea! The glorious sea!" shouted Hare, dancing to the door of the caravan.

Grey Rabbit and the others hurried out, laughing and cheering as they saw the wide green sea with the little snowy waves, curling in the distance.

"Unharness me," said Duke, turning his head. "There's a sandy cove below the cliffs. Go and enjoy yourselves and come back when the sun goes down to bathe."

They collected their belongings and ran down the narrow track to the sea.

When they reached the bottom they all gave little shrieks of joy. They felt the warm sand under their feet, and the strong sea air in their fur and feathers.

They stood looking at the vast stretch of water, and they saw the little curling waves, each edged with white lace like Grey Rabbit's best petticoat.

"What does the sea talk about?" asked Fuzzypeg, holding tight to Grey Rabbit's hand. He was rather frightened by the little waves that rolled up to his feet.

"Sea breezes. Sea breezes. No more of your sneezes," whispered the sea.

Hare picked up a strand of seaweed, but the waves came up and washed his feet. With a wild cry he ran away, but when he looked round the sea also had turned back.

"It keeps coming and going," said he, puzzled.

There were several strangers on the beach.

A flock of snowy seagulls walked on the sand, and a black cormorant sat fishing from a rock.

"Grey Rabbit, Grey Rabbit," sang the little curling waves as they lapped at Grey Rabbit's soft little feet, and touched her grey dress.

The sea wind blew her apron like a sail, and tugged at her petticoat. It pulled Hare's red coat, and ruffled Squirrel's tail. It nipped Mr Hedgehog's nose, and tossed Fuzzypeg's smock over his head.

"Wise Owl said the sea would take our tishoos away, but I'm going to sneeze," announced Grey Rabbit. Hare and Squirrel both wrinkled up their noses, as they felt a sneeze coming.

"A-tishoo! A-tishoo! A-tishoo!" they all sneezed together. The breeze caught those sneezes and tossed them up in the air. They floated away like baby clouds in the blue sky.

"My tishoo has gone," cried Grey Rabbit. "I'm quite well! Hurray!"

"Mine's gone too," added Squirrel.

"Hurray! Both my tishoos have flown away!" laughed Hare, and the three animals danced on the sand, waving their paws.

Then Grey Rabbit lifted up her grey skirt and paddled in the sea. Fuzzypeg joined her. He was so small a wave might have upset him, so he held tight to her apron.

Water Rat took off his velvet coat and white ruffles and swam in the shallow water. Hare plucked up his courage, took off his red coat and rushed into the sea, and then out again, as he saw a wave coming.

Squirrel, with a cockleshell tied on her head for a hat and a garland of seaweed round her neck, began to dance on the edge of the sea, and Moldy Warp dug a tunnel and made a mole heap.

Suddenly there was a shout from the Hedgehogs. And the Speckledy Hen cackled from her nest of pebbles.

"Thief! Robber! Bandit!" they called.

A seagull flew away with Hare's red coat and a second gull took Water Rat's frills. The birds flew to a rocky part of the cliff, where they dropped their treasures by their nests, with loud squawks to their wives and babies.

"Fine bedcovers," they cried.

The group of little animals on the beach could see the red coat and white ruffles hanging far above them on the wild rocky cliff.

"Who is going to get them back?" asked Hare, dancing with rage.

"I'll go," said Grey Rabbit.

"And I," added Squirrel.

"Then I'll go and take care of you," said Hare.

So the three little animals climbed the high dangerous rocks, and Squirrel on her nimble feet was always the first. She swung up the gorse bushes, and skipped over the cracks. Hare leapt up and down, rushing forward and then stopping in alarm. Grey Rabbit plodded silently along behind them. Squirrel arrived first at the ledge where the seagulls' nests lay.

Little grey gulls were toddling about, but when Squirrel came near the mother gulls pecked fiercely at her head. Luckily Squirrel wore the cockleshell hat she had picked up on the beach, and this protected her.

"Oh! Oh!" screamed the gulls. "You have a very hard head."

"I want Hare's coat and Water Rat's frills," said Squirrel, trembling with fright.

Then Hare's head popped round the corner and Grey Rabbit's startled little face appeared.

The gulls swooped at them, but Grey Rabbit shook her apron in their faces, and Hare gave a queer shrill cry, remarkably like Wise Owl's call.

"Too-whit! Too-whee-ee-ee! The horrible sea!" he hooted.

The noise frightened the gulls away for a moment, and the three seized the red coat and the torn snowy frills, and ran off, tumbling, rolling, tearing their fur, scratching their legs, as they fell down the cliff to their friends at the bottom.

"Never make friends with a wild seagull," said Fuzzypeg solemnly.

Hare put on his coat. Squrriel combed her tail. Grey Rabbit pulled thorns from her fur and bathed her cut feet.

Mrs Hedgehog lighted a fire of driftwood, and they filled the kettle from a stream that ran down the rocks.

Then, with the bright fire crackling, and the good tea brewing, and the food spread out, they enjoyed the picnic and forgot their troubles.

"Now for a sand pie," said Hare, when all the food was eaten. He filled his bucket with sand, and the rest watched, for Hare was sometimes very clever at doing things. He patted the top firm, and turned it upside down. He looked round at his audience, and then he slowly lifted the bucket.

There was a lovely golden pie, as nice to look at as Grey Rabbit's sponge pudding!

They all had a taste, but nobody liked it very much. Hare was so proud of his first pie he made another and another, until he had a ring of them. Squirrel put a cockleshell on each turret, Grey Rabbit draped seaweed about them, and little Fuzzypeg found pebbles to adorn them.

Hare leapt over them, and Fuzzypeg followed, crying, "Follow my leader," but nobody could jump high like Hare.

They wandered along the sandy strip, and all was quiet except for the music of the waves. They found beautiful pebbles, and pearly shells. Grey Rabbit picked up a starfish and Squirrel found a mermaid's purse.

Hare found a long razor-shell, Fuzzypeg gathered a lot of seaweed balloons, and Water Rat discovered a sea urchin, prickly as Mr Hedgehog himself.

So the happy day passed, and the sun moved down to the sea to bathe in a flood of gold.

"What time is it, Hare?" asked Grey Rabbit.

Hare looked at his watch. The fingers pointed as usual to twelve o'clock. The watch had not kept time since Hare once stirred his tea with it. He dipped the watch in the sea and listened.

"Tick Tack, time to go back," said the fat little watch, and the fingers began to move again. "The sea has cured my watch too," cried Hare.

They put the starfish in the bucket which they half filled with water, so that the tide would not flow over the edge. They twined seaweed round their necks, and stuffed their pockets with striped pebbles. Then, waving goodbye to the sea, they wandered wearily up the steep narrow track.

"Hurry up," cried Duke, who was expecting them. "The sun is getting into the sea."

Far away they saw a golden track on the water, like a pathway in the waves.

Hare fastened the horse's traces, and clambered inside the caravan.

Everyone got into the bed, and nobody bothered to drive.

The horse jogged along the lanes, and the first stars pricked the evening sky. Inside the caravan all was quiet, for every little animal was fast asleep.

They reached the common at midnight without any more adventures, and, yawning, they tumbled out on the grass. Grey Rabbit locked the door and Hare unharnessed the horse. The gipsy lay under a bush wrapped in a coat, snoring, so after whispering their thanks to Duke they all hurried away.

The Speckledy Hen flew over the fields.

Moldy Warp went underground to his home.

Water Rat ran swiftly to the river. Mr and Mrs Hedgehog with a sleepy little Fuzzypeg went slowly to the cottage.

Squirrel, Hare and Little Grey Rabbit ran along the field paths, with many a backward look. They found their key, and entered the house, and went to bed.

"Seabreezes. Seabreezes," murmured Grey Rabbit, as she curled up under the blanket. "I like the seabreezes."

In the morning the gipsy opened his eyes and stared at the caravan. He unlocked the door and looked suspiciously around. A necklace of seaweed hung from a hook, a heap of shells lay on the rumpled bed. Little footprints were everywhere. In a mug was a golden guinea.

"Real gold," said he, biting it. "Now I wonder who took this caravan!"

Duke never said a word. He went on nibbling the grass, and laughing softly to himself over the adventure.

Water Rat's Picnic

ONE DAY Water Rat came out of his house by the riverside.
The garden was full of riverbank flowers, bright blue
forget-me-nots, yellow flags and water-mint.

Water Rat whistled a sea-shanty and went towards his
boathouse. There lay the *Saucy Nancy*, the neatest, prettiest little
boat you ever saw! She had a pair of slender oars like scarlet
wings. A couple of cushions lay on the seat, and a water jar
was in the bow. Water Rat was very proud of his boat.

On this particular fine day Water Rat had packed a picnic basket.

"Where might you be going today, Sir?" asked Mrs Webster, his housekeeper.

"I'm going to invite some young friends of mine on a water-picnic," said Water Rat happily. "They've never seen a boat, I believe."

Water Rat settled himself in the boat and paddled peacefully upstream. Green dragonflies darted here and there, and a kingfisher shot by like a blue arrow. At the water's edge a brown water hen was busy with a heap of washing.

"A good drying day," said Water Rat, and the water hen looked up from her work.

"The ducks are very tiresome," she complained. "They tease me and carry off the washing."

"Never mind, you've got a fine young family to help you," said Water Rat.

A crowd of fluffy water chicks danced on the ripples. "Fourteen children," said the water hen proudly, "and every one of them is a champion swimmer."

Water Rat took up the oars and rowed some distance.
He moored the boat to the roots of a willow and leapt out.
Then he walked across the fields to Grey Rabbit's house.
He tapped at the door.

"Come in! Come in!" called Grey Rabbit, who was busy
making strawberry jam.

"Oh, Water Rat! How pleased I am to see you!" she cried.
"Do sit down. I shan't be long now. The strawberries are
bubbling."

"Nice smell," said Water Rat, sinking into the rocking-
chair and wiping his forehead. "We have no strawberries by
the river."

"What kind of jam do you make?" asked Grey Rabbit.

"Lily-bud jam," said Water Rat.

Grey Rabbit ladled the jam into a row of little glass jars, and covered each with a strawberry leaf.

"I came to invite you and Squirrel to go for a picnic," said Water Rat. "My boat is moored by the old willow and the food is aboard."

"A picnic! A boat!" cried Little Grey Rabbit.

"A boat? A real live boat?" called Squirrel, dancing in on tiptoes.

"A picnic? A real live picnic?" shouted Hare, popping his head in at the window.

"I'm afraid my boat will only hold three," said Water Rat coldly.

Hare came into the room and stood in front of Water Rat.

"Look here," he cried. "Do you mean to say you are going on a picnic without me? It's impossible! What is there to eat, Water Rat?"

"Egg and cress sandwiches, marigold sponge, watermint jellies—"

"Stop! Stop!" moaned Hare.

"I'm afraid we can't go, Water Rat. We can't leave Hare behind," said Squirrel.

"I have a plan," said Water Rat. "Suppose you race along the river bank, Hare, while I row Grey Rabbit and Squirrel. Then you can choose the place for the picnic and we will all have a feast under the trees."

"That's a good idea!" said Hare. "It isn't the boat I want, but the picnic."

"That's settled then." Water Rat breathed again.

They shut their windows and locked the door, and put the key under the mat. Grey Rabbit carried a pot of strawberry jam, Hare his fishing net and Squirrel a pretty little sunshade. They tripped along by Water Rat's side, asking about the boat.

"Oh! how beautiful!" cried Grey Rabbit, when she saw the *Saucy Nancy* under the willow branches.

"You shall steer, Grey Rabbit," said Water Rat, "and Squirrel shall sit on a cushion."

He helped them both into the boat and untied the rope.

"Look at the waves, and the darting fishes, and the green weeds!" cried Grey Rabbit. She jumped with excitement as she saw the water so near.

Squirrel twirled her new sunshade, and glanced at her reflection in the clear river.

"Goodbye. Goodbye," called Hare. "I shall meet you soon. Take care of the food and don't fall in the river."

He galloped along the bank and they waved their paws to him. Soon he was out of sight.

Water Rat rowed with light, graceful sweeps of the scarlet oars. They saw a green frog sitting among the water-buttercups with a little fishing rod and a woven bag to hold his catch.

They stopped to chat with the water hen, and admired the fourteen little chicks which swam squeaking round the boat.

The little water hens scrambled along the oars and climbed on Grey Rabbit's knee, poking their beaks in her apron pocket.

"Come away, you naughty children," scolded their mother. Grey Rabbit stroked their tiny brown heads before she lifted them back into the water.

There was a scurry and flurry, and a loud quacking as a flock of white ducks came hurrying up. The ducks swam up to the boat, diving and pushing.

"Where are you going?" they asked

"For a picnic," said Water Rat. "Don't come too near! You shake my boat."

One duck snatched Squirrel's sunshade and carried it off, laughing. Another pulled the strings of Grey Rabbit's little blue apron and swam away with it on her shoulders. Another twitched the ribbon from Squirrel's tail and a fourth seized the pot of strawberry jam.

There was such a commotion, such a rocking of the boat and a splash of water that nobody noticed another duck seize the picnic basket.

"Oh! Oh!" cried Grey Rabbit and Squirrel.

"It is outrageous!" said Water Rat. He stared at one of the ducks. "Is it possible? Has she taken the picnic basket?"

The duck held the little basket, and tried to open it. As she struggled, the basket slipped and went down, down to the bottom of the river.

"I'll get it," muttered Water Rat. He took off his velvet coat and dived overboard. Down to the bed of the river he went, and among the waterweeds he found the basket. He put his arms round it and swam back to the boat. He hauled it over the side and clambered after it. Then he rowed as fast as he could, away from the ducks.

"Luckily it's lined with mackintosh," said Water Rat. "It won't be any the worse. But I'm sorry about your apron, Grey Rabbit, and your sunshade, Squirrel."

"I will make another apron," said Grey Rabbit, cheerfully.

"And I will have one of those big round leaves for a sunshade if you will pick it for me, Water Rat," said Squirrel.

Water Rat picked the lily leaf and Squirrel held it over her head and tried to forget her sunshade.

"Where's Hare?" asked Water Rat, staring at the river bank. "He ought to be waiting for us."

"Coo-oo," called Grey Rabbit. "Coo-oo, Hare."

"Coo-oo," came a faint reply.

Water Rat pulled the boat to the shore. From out of the reeds peered Hare, his coat torn and his net broken.

"Oh dear!" he cried. "I've been chased by a dog and tossed by a bull and bitten by gnats. And you've been rowing peacefully on the river."

"Not so peacefully," laughed Grey Rabbit. "I've lost my blue apron, Hare."

"And I've lost my sunshade," added Squirrel, leaping lightly out of the boat.

"And we nearly lost the picnic basket," said Water Rat.

"That would have been a calamity," muttered Hare. "A cal-cal-calamity!" He took the basket from Water Rat and clasped it to his heart.

Grey Rabbit and Squirrel ran about picking up sticks, and Water Rat carried the kettle and water jar to the hollow by the trees.

"Make a big fire!" called Hare. Water Rat struck a light. The fire crackled and yellow flames shot up. Squirrel balanced the kettle on top.

"Come along, Hare. You have more breath than any of us," said Squirrel.

Hare puffed out his cheeks and blew like the wind. Soon the kettle began to sing in its high shrill voice.

Water Rat unfastened the picnic basket.

Hare leapt for joy when he saw the patties and sandwiches and jellies in their waterproof wrappers. What a feast there was! They laughed and sang and told their adventures, and quite forgot their troubles.

Hare was very hungry, for, he explained, he had run for miles, while they had been resting in the boat. "I was tossed by a gnat and bitten by a bull," said he, as he took the last sandwich.

"Bitten by a bulrush, you mean," said Water Rat.

They took the cups to the river edge and washed them and dried them on the grasses. They repacked the basket, then they sat down among the daisies to watch the river whirling below them.

Hare crept softly out of sight, and climbed into the boat. He untied the rope and pushed her into the stream.

"You didn't know I could row," he called, splashing with the scarlet oars. "It's quite easy."

"Oh Hare! Take care!" shrieked Squirrel, as the boat rocked dangerously.

"Sit down, Hare," said Water Rat. "You'll upset her if you stand up."

"Your boat is so wobbly," said Hare, swaying to one side. "Steady on there! Steady!"

Hare sat down with a thump, and the boat shook.

He dipped the oars deep in the river and dragged up some weeds. Then the oars waved wildly, Hare's feet flew up, and he shot backwards into the water.

"Save me! Save me! I'm drowning!" he cried, kicking and struggling.

Out of the shadows came the ducks, one with the blue apron on her shoulders, another with the red sunshade above her head.

They circled round Hare and grabbed him by his fur. One took his left ear and another his right, another his leg and the fourth his coat tail. Then they swam to the shore with him.

They pushed him on the bank and away they went, cackling with laughter.

Squirrel and Grey Rabbit dried him with their handkerchiefs and squeezed the water out of his fur. The poor bedraggled Hare crouched over the fire, shivering.

"It's very wet in the river," he said. "I never knew that boat wasn't safe."

"You will have to run all the way home," said Grey Rabbit. "It will keep you from catching cold."

Water Rat swam after the little boat and the pair of oars which were floating down the river. He rowed back, dried the boat and wiped the cushions.

"I'm going home!" said Hare crossly. "I feel a chill in my bones." He started off along the river bank, trotting with head bent.

The others seated themselves in the boat, but Water Rat turned to Grey Rabbit.

"Would you like to see my house?" he asked. "It is quite near. There's watercress in my stream and I'll give you some to take home."

Grey Rabbit and Squirrel were delighted, and Water Rat turned the boat up the stream and stopped at the boathouse at the bottom of the garden. They walked up the garden path and entered the damp little house.

One a table in the hall stood an aquarium with duckweed and stickleback and minnows.

"Chirrup! Chirrup!" whistled Water Rat, and the tiny fish came swimming to the side of the tank and held up their noses.

Squirrel could hardly tear herself away from this watery scene, but Water Rat led the way to the parlour. It was very wet, and Squirrel tucked her feet high as she sat on the bulrush chair.

"Mrs Webster, will you bring some of your water-lily jam for my guests?" asked Water Rat.

Grey Rabbit and Squirrel smiled at the stout old water rat, and Mrs Webster fetched the little pots of lily jam and packed them in a bag for Grey Rabbit to carry.

"I'll get the watercress," said Water Rat.

"Oh, Miss Grey Rabbit and Miss Squirrel!" said Mrs Webster. "I am glad to see you! And how is Mister Hare? I suppose he couldn't go to the picnic, being too big for the boat?"

"Oh dear!" cried Grey Rabbit. "I'd forgotten about him! He fell in the river, Mrs Webster. We must hurry home."

"Hum! Always doing something, Mister Hare. Played noughts and crosses with the Fox, didn't he?" Mrs Webster smoothed her apron placidly.

Water Rat came padding back with a basket of green cresses.

"We must go home," said Grey Rabbit, as she thanked him. "Poor Hare is waiting for us, all wet."

"Goodbye, Mrs Webster. Goodbye," they called, as they hurried away.

Water Rat rowed swiftly, and soon they were back at the old willow tree.

"Thank you, dear Water Rat. Thank you," they said, and they scampered home.

"Hare! Hare!" they called as they went into the house. "Guess what we did! We went to Water Rat's house and we saw – Hare, where are you?"

A violent sneeze shook the house. They ran upstairs to Hare's bedroom.

"A-tishoo!" sneezed Hare. "I thought you were both drowned! A-tishoo!"

Squirrel and Grey Rabbit raced round with herbs and hot water and soon Hare was snug in bed with a teapot of elderflower tea.

"Now, tell me all about it," said he.

So Little Grey Rabbit began to tell of Mrs Webster and the aquarium. Her silvery little voice went on with her tale, but Hare shut his eyes. He was lulled by the sound, and before she had finished he was fast asleep. She tiptoed downstairs and joined Squirrel who was resting by the fire.

Pit-pat! Pit-pat! Little footsteps came flipping to the door. Then there was muffled laughter, and a shuffle and flop.

Grey Rabbit looked at Squirrel, and Squirrel looked at Grey Rabbit. Then, Pit-pat! Pitter-pat! Little footsteps went flipping down the garden path, flip-flopping over the grass. Quack! Quack!

Little Grey Rabbit stepped softly to the door and opened it. On the doorstep lay her blue apron, rather torn and dirty, and very wet.

"Oh, how glad I am to get my little apron again," she cried, and she hung it by the fire to dry.

But the sunshade never came back. The ducks liked it so much they wouldn't part with it. Any day you could see them swimming down the river, one of them carrying Squirrel's sunshade, and another playing with her ribbon bow.

Autumn

Fuzzypeg Goes
to School

IT WAS BEDTIME, and little Fuzzypeg the Hedgehog sat by the fire in his nightgown eating his bread and milk. His mother was mending his blue smock which he had torn on his prickles.

"Will my father tell me a tale tonight?" asked Fuzzypeg.

"If you're a good hedgehog and eat every bit of your supper," said Mrs Hedgehog kindly.

Old Hedgehog came into the cosy room.

"Please tell me a bedtime story," implored Fuzzypeg.

"Wait a minute," said Old Hedgehog, and he scratched his head, trying to think of a nice tale.

Then he began to sing:

> *A Frog he would a-wooing go,*
> *Whether his mother would let him or no,*
> *Heigh-ho! says Rowley.*

Fuzzypeg beat time with the spoon on the wooden bowl, and
Mrs Hedgehog forgot to thread her needle as she listened.

"What a lovely tale!" cried Fuzzypeg.

"I larned that in my schooldays, when I was a youngster,"
said Hedgehog, modestly.

"Can I go to school and learn poems?" asked Fuzzypeg.

"I think he's big enough, don't you, Hedgehog?"
And Mrs Hedgehog looked at her husband.

"Yes. It's about time he had some eddication," replied Hedgehog. "You can't get on without Wisdom. Just think what a lot Wise Owl knows!"

"Can I go to school tomorrow? Please! Please!" Fuzzypeg asked, jumping down from his stool.

"Yes, if I've mended these holes in time," Mrs Hedgehog told him.

Fuzzypeg hopped round the room for joy. Then he went to say goodnight to the world.

"Goodnight, Moon," he called to the delicate crescent moon in the sky, and a whispering voice came through the air, "Goodnight, Fuzzypeg."

"Goodnight, Star," he called to the evening star, and it nodded goodnight.

The next morning Fuzzypeg awoke early.

"I'm going to school today," he sang, and he rolled downstairs in a prickly ball.

Old Hedgehog had been out since dawn, milking the cows.

Fuzzypeg saw him returning and ran to meet him. The hedgehog carried something under his arm and Fuzzypeg danced round, asking what it was.

"Don't be in such a hurry," said Old Hedgehog, smiling. He gave Mrs Hedgehog the milk for breakfast, then he sat down and opened the parcel, taking from the leafy paper a little leather bag.

"A school bag!" cried Fuzzypeg excitedly. "A school bag! Where has it come from?"

There was a big pocket for sandwiches, two little ones for lesson books and a tiny one for the penny to pay for the schooling.

"Grey Rabbit gave it to me when she heard you were going to school," said Hedgehog.

"I took the milk as usual this morning, and tells her, 'My Fuzzypeg's going to get Wisdom same as Wise Owl.' 'Wait a minute, Hedgehog,' sez she. So I stood on the doorstep, and then Grey Rabbit comes downstairs, carrying this.

"'A lesson bag for Fuzzypeg,' sez she."

"What shall I put in it?" asked Fuzzypeg.

"Your lessons – sums and poems and tales," said Hedgehog, "your sandwiches for elevenses, and your penny for the schoolmaster."

Then they all had a good breakfast, and Fuzzypeg started off for school with the leather bag on his back.

"Don't be late," said his mother, as she waved goodbye.

As Fuzzypeg went down the lane he saw his cousins, Tim and Bill Hedgehog.

"Hello, Fuzzypeg!" they called. "Where are you going with that fine bag?"

"I'm going to school," said Fuzzypeg proudly.

"Wait a minute. We'll come too," cried the little hedgehogs, and they ran to their mother.

"Mother! Mother!" they shouted excitedly. "Can we go to school with Fuzzypeg?"

"Yes. If Fuzzypeg is big enough, so are you," said their mother.

She brushed their quills and cut their sandwiches, and sent them off.

"Be quick," called Fuzzypeg, "or we'll be late."

"Late? What's late?" asked Tim.

"I don't know. Something we musn't be," replied Fuzzypeg.

They trotted along the lane, when who should they see but Hare, lolloping along in his bright blue coat.

"Hello, Fuzzypeg! Hello, young 'uns!" he called. "What's inside your bag, Fuzzypeg?" he asked.

"Sandwiches," said Fuzzypeg, and he brought them out and divided them.

"Now you have plenty of room for other things," said Hare, and they gathered bindweed, forget-me-nots and foxgloves.

"Those are all lessons," said Hare. "Now I will teach you your A B C.

"A. Hay grows in the Daisy Field, when the sun shines," Hare said.

"B. Bees live in gardens. They get honey and that is a good thing."

"C. Seas are very wet. They are all water and they never dry up."

"That's all for today. You know your A B C," said Hare, suddenly running off, for he had spied Little Grey Rabbit coming towards them.

When she saw the three little hedgehogs sitting on the grass, Little Grey Rabbit was astonished.

"What are you doing here, Fuzzypeg?" she asked.
"I thought you were at school. Now run along as fast as you can, or your teacher will be very cross."

So off they ran, under the gate to the Daisy Field, and across the meadow to the little pasture where Jonathan Rabbit had his school.

A sweet little tinkle tinkle came from the pasture.

"That's the school bell," said a thrush. "You'll be late. Young Hare always rings the harebells, you know. He's been jingling them a long time now."

So they ran, puffing and panting towards the sound of the bluebells, which floated like music from a house hidden in the gorse bushes.

"I've got a stitch in my side," groaned Bill, and he drank from a stream to cure it.

"I've cut my leg on a bramble," cried Tim, and he stopped to find a cobweb to bind up the wound.

"I've tored my smock on the gorse bush," said Fuzzypeg, and he looked for a thorn to pin it together.

In the distance the little hare stood in a grove of slender harebells, shaking the bells for the last time.

Then he ran into school, and there was silence.

The three hedgehogs raced to the school door. They pushed aside a leafy curtain, and knocked at the little green door with a brass knocker, hidden in the low bushes.

Then they entered a room whose walls were made of closely woven blackberry bushes and wild roses.

The floor was the soft turf of the pasture, and the ceiling of the schoolroom was the blue sky, where the sun was now shining. The little hedgehogs walked shyly across the room to old Jonathan.

"Benjamin Hedgehog. Timothy Hedgehog. Fuzzypeg Hedgehog," said he, writing their names on a rose leaf, in squiggly letters.

"Each of you is, 'A diller, a dollar, a ten-o'clock scholar.' Remember that school begins at nine o'clock, and don't be late!"

They sat down next to hedgehogs, squirrels, rabbits, the young hare, a small mole and some fieldmice. They all read from books made of green leaves which Jonathan gave them.

Then he asked them some questions, and all the little animals stood up in a row, with Fuzzypeg at the end.

"Which flower helps a rabbit to remember?" he asked.

Nobody knew the answer, but little Fuzzypeg drew the blue forget-me-nots from his bag and held them up.

"Quite right, Fuzzypeg. Go to the top of the class," said Jonathan.

"Which flower shuts its eyes when it rains?" he asked.

All the little animals shut their eyes and tried forget-me-notting, but Fuzzypeg held up the white trumpet of the climbing bindweed.

Then Jonathan asked his last question.

"Which flower makes gloves for cold paws?"

Every animal knew the answer, and they all shouted at the tops of their voices, "Foxgloves," before Fuzzypeg could get the purple foxglove from the bottom of his satchel.

"Now for a counting lesson," said Jonathan.

"One, two, buckle my shoe," sang the animals, and all the little hedgehogs fastened their shoes.

"Three, four, knock at the door," they sang, and they ran to knock on the brass knocker.

"Five, six, pick up sticks," they sang, and they all ran into the pasture to gather as many sticks as they could carry.

"Seven, eight, lay them straight," they sang, and each tried to lay his sticks in even lengths.

"Eleven o'clock," said Jonathan, blowing at a dandelion clock. "Go and eat your sandwiches."

Fuzzypeg had nothing to eat, but there was plenty of fun and he played leapfrog with the others up and down the soft grass.

Suddenly Fuzzypeg saw a little figure in a grey dress coming towards the school.

"Here's Little Grey Rabbit!" called all the animals, and they rushed to meet her, and begged her to tell them a story.

Little Grey Rabbit sat down in the shade of a hawthorn tree, and began the tale of Red Riding Hood. She had just got to the part where Red Riding Hood came to her grandmother's cottage, when there was a mighty roaring noise close by, from behind the hawthorn tree.

"Woof! Woof! Woof!" said a terrible voice.

"Oh! Oh!" they all shrieked. "Oh! the Wolf!"

And they all ran helter-skelter up and down the field.

Grey Rabbit stood very still, for she thought she recognised the voice.

"Boo! Boo! Woof! Woof! I'll nab you," roared the creature, gruffly.

"Come out, Hare," said Grey Rabbit sternly.

"Hare! Naughty Hare! Come out at once! I know that voice. You can't deceive *me*."

From behind the tree leaped Hare, holding a cone-shaped trumpet, made from the bark of a silver birch tree.

"Ha! Ha! I frightened you. You thought I was a Wolf, didn't you?"

All the little animals came creeping out, to stare at the trumpet which Hare carried; all, except Fuzzypeg.

"Where's Fuzzypeg?" asked Little Grey Rabbit.

"Where's Fuzzypeg?" echoed the others.

Then they heard a squeaky little voice.

"A-tishoo!" it said. "Help! A-tishoo! A-shoo!"

From out of the stream crawled a very bedraggled little hedgehog, all covered with water weeds.

"C is very wet," he said. "A-tishoo!"

"Poor little Fuzzypeg," said Grey Rabbit, running up to him. "You'd better go straight home to bed."

"School, dismissed!" shouted Jonathan.

All the little animals leaped up and down crying,
"A holiday!"

"I didn't want a holiday. I've only just begun,"
said Fuzzypeg in a quavering voice. "A-tishoo!"

But Grey Rabbit took him by the hand, and hurried
him home, while Hare ran alongside.

"I'll give you the trumpet, Fuzzypeg," said he. "Then you can be a wolf, or even a lion."

This cheered Fuzzypeg so much he forgot about missing school, and wetting his new school bag.

"Whatever have you been and gone and done?" asked Mrs Hedgehog, holding up her hands in horror when she saw her wet little son.

Little Grey Rabbit explained what had happened, and Hare said, "I'm very sorry, Mrs Hedgehog. It won't occur again." Then he ran off, leaping home.

"You must put Fuzzypeg to bed at once, Mrs Hedgehog," said Grey Rabbit.

So little Fuzzypeg was popped into his warm bed, with a bowl of delicious soup and blackcurrant tea.

Grey Rabbit sat at his bedside and she sang little songs to him while Fuzzypeg sneezed and sneezed again. On the wall hung the trumpet, and when Grey Rabbit blew it, a roaring noise came from it which made Fuzzypeg laugh.

When Little Grey Rabbit started for home, Fuzzypeg croaked, "Good-bye, Grey Rabbit."

And then he shut his eyes and slept till his father came home.

"What did they larn you besides swimming, my son?" asked Old Hedgehog, as he stood at the bedside looking at little Fuzzypeg, muffled up in his blankets.

"Hay, Bee and Sea. I think that was what Hare taught us. I fell into C, Father. And tomorrow we're going to learn, 'Here we go gathering nuts in May.' I like school, Father."

"You've not larned much," said Old Hedgehog, "and they say, 'A little larning is a dangerous thing.' You'd better get a bit more knowledge tomorrow, and don't go to Mr Hare for your lessons neither."

Winter

Little Grey Rabbit's Christmas

IT HAD BEEN SNOWING FOR HOURS. Hare stood in the garden of the little house at the end of the wood, watching the snowflakes tumbling down like white feathers from the grey sky.

"Whatever are you doing, Hare?" cried Squirrel, who was sitting close to the fire. "Come in! You'll catch cold."

"I am catching cold, and eating it too," replied Hare, happily.

"Hare! How long do you think Grey Rabbit will be? Can you see her coming? What is she doing?" called Squirrel again.

"She's at the market, buying a Christmas feast for all of us,"

replied Hare, and he caught an extra large snowflake on his red tongue.

As he spoke, a small stout animal came trudging up the lane, laden with a heavy basket and a string bag bulging with knobbly surprises. Straggling behind was a little snow-covered creature.

"There she is!" cried Hare, leaping forward. "Make the tea, Squirrel."

He ran down the path, and then stopped, disappointed. "It's only Mrs Hedgehog!" he muttered. "And Fuzzypeg," he added, as he recognised the little fellow.

"Have you seen Little Grey Rabbit?" asked Hare, as he leaned over the gate.

"I have indeed," said Mrs Hedgehog, resting her burden on the snow. "She was at the market along of me. Then she went to talk to Old Joe the Carpenter."

"What did she want with Joe?" asked Hare.

"Please Sir!" cried Fuzzypeg. "I knows, Sir. I knows what Grey Rabbit went to the Carpenter for."

"Sh-sh!" Mrs Hedgehog shook her head at her son. "You mustn't let the cat out of the bag." Then, picking up her basket, she continued on her way, with little Fuzzypeg protesting, "There wasn't a cat in the bag, Mother. There wasn't."

It was growing dark when Squirrel and Hare heard the sound of merry voices and the ringing of bells.

They ran to the door, and what should they see but a fine scarlet sledge drawn by two young rabbits, with Little Grey Rabbit herself sitting cosily on the top!

"Oh Grey Rabbit, what a lovely sledge!" cried Squirrel, and she rubbed her paws over the smooth sides.

"Grey Rabbit! Our names are on it!" shouted Hare.

He pointed excitedly to the words, 'Squirrel, Hare and Little Grey Rabbit' written round the sides. "It's ours. It says so!"

"Yes. It is our very own," said Grey Rabbit. "I ordered it from Old Joe, and these kind rabbits insisted on bringing me home."

After breakfast the next day, Squirrel and Grey Rabbit sat on the sledge, and Hare pulled them over the field.

They came to their favourite hill. Hare climbed on behind them, and stretched out his long legs.

"One to be ready!

"Two to be steady!

"Three to be off!" he cried, and away they went down the steep slope.

"Whoo-oo-oo!" cried Hare. "What a speed! Whoops! Whoa!"

But the sledge wouldn't stop.

At last it struck a mole-hill, and over they all toppled, head over heels.

"Sixty miles an hour!" cried Hare, sitting up and rubbing his elbow.

Little Fuzzypeg, carrying a slice of bread and jam, came to watch the fun. He stared at the three dragging their sledge up the slope.

"I want to toboggan," he said softly, but nobody heard. "Look at *me* toboggan! Watch *me*!" cried Fuzzypeg. He made himself into a ball and rolled down the hill, faster and faster. When he got to the bottom there was no Fuzzypeg to be seen, only an enormous snowball.

"What a big snowball!" cried Squirrel, climbing off the sledge.

"What a beauty!" exclaimed Grey Rabbit.

"Help! Help!" squeaked a tiny voice. "Get me out!"

"What's that?" cried Squirrel.

"Help! Help!" piped Fuzzypeg.

"That's a talking snowball," said Hare. "Isn't that interesting? I shall take it home and keep it in the garden."

He dragged the large ball on to the sledge and pulled the load uphill. When he reached the top, Hare rolled the ball to the ground and gave it a kick.

"Ugh!" he cried, limping. "There's a thorn inside."

"Help! Help!" shrieked the tiny faraway voice. "Lemme out!"

"That sounds like Fuzzypeg," said Grey Rabbit, and she bent over and loosened the caked snow.

Out came the little hedgehog, eating his bread and jam.

"However did you get inside a snowball?" asked Hare.

"I didn't get inside. It got round me," replied Fuzzypeg. "Can I go on your sledge now?"

Hare took the little hedgehog for a ride, but when Fuzzypeg flung his arms round Hare's waist, he sprang shrieking away.

"That's enough," he said. "My motto is, 'Never go hedging with a sledgehog'. I mean to say, 'Never go sledging with a hedgehog'."

Fuzzypeg ran home and returned with a tea tray. After him came a crowd of rabbits, each carrying a tray, and they all rode helter-skelter down the slope, shouting and laughing as they tried to race each other.

Squirrel, Hare and Little Grey Rabbit took their sledge to Moldy Warp's house. Squirrel ran up the holly trees and gathered sprigs of the blazing red berries. The mole came out and showed them the mistletoe growing on an oak tree. And then he helped them to tie their branches on the sledge.

They said goodbye and hurried home.

Hare shut the sledge in the woodshed and carried the holly and mistletoe indoors. Grey Rabbit stood at the table making mince pies, while Hare and Squirrel decorated the room. They popped sprigs on the clock, over the corner cupboard, round the warming pan and on the dresser.

Little Grey Rabbit looked up from her patty-pans and waved her rolling pin to direct operations.

Up the lane came a little group, carrying rolls of music and pipes of straw. They talked softly as they walked up to the closed door of Grey Rabbit's house. They arranged themselves in a circle, they coughed and cleared their throats and held up their music to the moonlight.

"Now then, altogether!" cried an important-looking rabbit, playing a note on his straw pipe. "One, two, three!" and with their noses in the air they began to sing in small squeaky voices this Christmas carol:

Holly red and mistletoe white,
The stars are shining with golden light,
Burning like candles this Holy Night,
Holly red and mistletoe white.

"Hush! What's that noise?" cried Hare, dropping his mistletoe.

"It's carollers!" said Grey Rabbit, and she held up her wooden spoon.

They flung wide the door and saw the little group of rabbits and hedgehogs, peering at their sheets of music.

"Come in! Come in!" cried Grey Rabbit. "Come and sing by the fireside. You look frozen with the cold."

"We're all right," said a big rabbit, "but a warm drink would wet our whistles."

Grey Rabbit took the two-handled Christmas mug of primrose wine from the fire, and the carollers passed it round.

Then they stood by the hearth and sang all the songs they knew: 'The moon shines bright', 'I saw three ships a-sailing', and 'Green grows the holly'.

"Now we must be off," they said, when Grey Rabbit had given them hot mince pies. "We have to sing at all the rabbit houses tonight. Goodnight. Happy Christmas!"

Squirrel, Hare and Little Grey Rabbit stood watching the carollers as they crossed the fields, listening to 'Holly red and mistletoe white', which the animals sang as they trotted along.

"I think I shall take the sledge and toboggan down the hill by moonlight," said Hare.

He seized the cord of the sledge and ran across the fields, and up the hill.

Then down he swooped, flying like a bird.

Again and again he rushed down, his eyes on the lovely moon. Suddenly he noticed a dark shadow running alongside. It was his own shadow, but Hare saw the long ears of a monster.

"Oh dear! Oh dear! Who is that fellow racing by my side?" he cried.

He took to his heels and hurried home, leaving the sledge lying in the field.

"Did you come without the sledge?" asked Squirrel. "Hare, you are a coward! I don't believe there was anybody at all."

"You ran away from your shadow. You've lost our lovely sledge!"

"Better than losing my lovely life," retorted Hare. He felt rather miserable. "I suppose we had better go to bed," he muttered. "I don't suppose there will be any presents tomorrow. I don't think Santa Claus will find this house with so much snow about!"

He went upstairs gloomily, but he hung up his furry stocking all the same, and so did Squirrel.

When all was quiet Grey Rabbit slipped out of bed. Under her bed was a store of parcels.

She opened them and filled the stockings with sugar-plums and lollipops. Then she ran downstairs to the kitchen, where the dying fire flickered softly.

She tied together sprays of holly and made a round ball called a kissing bunch. Then she hung it from a hook in the ceiling.

On Christmas morning Grey Rabbit was so sleepy she didn't wake up till Hare burst into her room.

"Grey Rabbit! Merry Christmas! He's been! Wake up! He's been in the night!"

"Who?" cried Grey Rabbit.

"Santa Claus!" cried Hare. "Be quick! Come downstairs and see."

Grey Rabbit dressed hurriedly and entered the kitchen.

"Look at the kissing bunch!" said Hare. "Isn't it lovely! Let's all kiss under it."

So they gave their Christmas morning kisses under the round Christmas bunch.

Robin the postman flew to the door with some Christmas cards and a letter. The little bird rested and ate some breakfast while Hare examined the letter.

"It's from Moldy Warp," he said.

"Yes, I know," replied Robin. "He gave it to me."

"You're reading it upside down, Hare!" cried Squirrel. She took the little letter and read, "Come tonight. Love from Moldy Warp."

"It's a party!" cried Hare. "Quick, Grey Rabbit! Write and say we'll come."

Grey Rabbit sat at her desk and wrote on an ivy leaf, "Thank you dear Moldy Warp."

Then away flew Robin with the leaf in his bag.

All day they enjoyed themselves, playing musical chairs, pulling tiny crackers, crunching lollipops.

They all trooped to the hill to look for the sledge, but it wasn't there. Snow had covered all traces of footprints.

"Santa Claus has borrowed it," said Grey Rabbit. "When the snow melts we shall find it."

When the first star appeared in the sky, the three animals wrapped themselves up in warm clothes, and set off for Moldy Warp's house. They carried presents for the lonely mole, and some of their own Christmas feast.

"What a pity you lost our sledge. We could have ridden on it tonight," said Squirrel to Hare.

When the three got near Moldy Warp's house they saw something glittering. A lighted tree grew by the path.

"Oh dear! Something's on fire!" cried Hare. "Let's put it out."

"Hush!" whispered Grey Rabbit. "It's a magical tree."

On every branch of the tree, candles wavered their tongues of flame. On the ground under the branches were bowls of hazel nuts, round loaves of bread, piles of cakes, small sacks of corn. There were jars of honey as big as thimbles, and bottles of heather ale.

"What do you think of my tree?" asked Moldy Warp, stepping out of the shadows.

"Is it a Fairy Tree?" asked Grey Rabbit.

"It's a Christmas tree," replied the mole. "It's for all the birds and beasts of the woods and fields. Now sit quietly and watch."

Across the snowy fields padded little creatures, all filled with curiosity to see the glowing tree.

"Help yourselves," cried Moldy Warp, waving his short arms. "It's Christmas. Eat and drink and warm yourselves."

From behind a tree Rat sidled towards Grey Rabbit.

"Miss Grey Rabbit," said he. "I found a scarlet sledge in the field last night, and as your family name was on it, I took the liberty of bringing it here."

"Oh, thank you, kind Rat," cried Grey Rabbit, clapping her paws. "The sledge is found! Come Hare! Squirrel! Moldy Warp!"

The scarlet sledge was clean and bright and on the top was a fleecy shawl. From under it Grey Rabbit drew three objects. The first was a walking stick made of holly wood. The second was a little wooden spoon. The third was a tiny box, and when Grey Rabbit opened the lid there was a little thimble inside which exactly fitted her.

"I've never had a thimble since Wise Owl swallowed mine," she said happily.

"Good Santa Claus," cried Hare. "He knew what we wanted."

"Only one person could make such delicate carvings," said Grey Rabbit.

"And that is Rat," said Squirrel.

"Three cheers for Rat!" cried Fuzzypeg, and they all cheered, "Hip! Hip! Hooray!"

Squirrel and Grey Rabbit climbed on the sledge, and Hare drew them over the snow.

"Goodnight. A happy Christmas!" they called.

"The same to you," answered Moldy Warp. The Hedgehog family waved and shouted, "Merry Christmas!"

"Heigh-ho! I'm sleepy," murmured Squirrel, "but it has been lovely. Thank you everyone for a happy day."

She curled down under the fleecy shawl by Grey Rabbit's side, clutching her wooden spoon. Grey Rabbit sat wide awake, her thimble was on her finger, her eyes shone with happiness.

Hare ran swiftly over the frozen snow, drawing the scarlet sledge towards the little house at the end of the wood:

Mistletoe white and holly red,
The day is over, we're off to bed,
Tired body and sleepy head,
Mistletoe white and holly red.

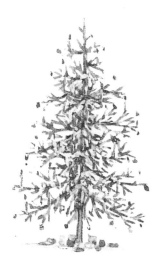

The End

A TEMPLAR BOOK

sed in the UK in 2015 by Templar Publishing,
an imprint of Bonnier Publishing Group,
Deepdene Lodge, Deepdene Avenue, Dorking, Surrey, RH5 4AT, UK
www.templarco.co.uk

Hare and the Easter Eggs:
Original edition published in the UK
in 1952 by William Collins Sons & Co

Little Grey Rabbit's May Day:
Original edition published in the UK
in 1963 by William Collins Sons & Co

Little Grey Rabbit Goes to the Sea:
Original edition published in the UK
in 1954 by William Collins Sons & Co

Water Rat's Picnic:
Original edition published in the UK
in 1943 by William Collins Sons & Co

Fuzzypeg Goes to School:
Original edition published in the UK
in 1938 by William Collins Sons & Co

Little Grey Rabbit's Christmas:
Original edition published in the UK
in 1939 by William Collins Sons & Co

Text copyright © 2015 by the Alison Uttley Literary Property Trust
Illustrations copyright © 2015 by the Estate of Margaret Tempest
Design copyright © 2015 by Templar Publishing
Leaves and snowflake vector shapes designed by Freepik.com

1 3 5 7 9 10 8 6 4 2

All rights reserved

ISBN 978-1-78370-261-9

Designed by Nathalie Eyraud
Edited by Susan Dickinson and Katie Haworth

Printed in Malaysia